Then There Was JESUS

An interactive Christmas story

written by:
DENA BAKER

tate publishing
CHILDREN'S DIVISION

Published by Tate Publishing & Enterprises, LLC
127 E. Trade Center Terrace | Mustang, Oklahoma 73064 USA
1.888.361.9473 | www.tatepublishing.com

Tate Publishing is committed to excellence in the publishing industry. The company reflects the philosophy established by the founders, based on Psalm 68:11,
"The Lord gave the word and great was the company of those who published it."

Book design copyright © 2014 by Tate Publishing, LLC. All rights reserved.
Cover and interior design by Rhezette Fiel
Illustrations by Jason Hutton

Published in the United States of America

ISBN: 978-1-63122-751-6
1. Juvenile Fiction / Holidays & Celebrations / Christmas & Advent
2. Juvenile Fiction / General
14.04.22

Dedication

To my grandchildren—Meg, Brad, Lyric, AJ, Daniel, Rachael, Morgan, and Serena.

Our Christmas Tradition

When celebrating Christmas each year, we as a family have developed a tradition that has become part of our family time every year. It has kept our focus on the true meaning of the Christmas celebration.

When our grandchildren were small, we used our nativity set to set up our Christmas display. Each family member was given a piece of the nativity set, and after the story of each piece was read, each would place that piece on the mantle in the appropriate spot.

After the nativity set was complete, my husband read the Christmas story in its entirety.

As the grandchildren grew older, a more grown-up version of the narration was developed, but the children's version remained everybody's favorite.

The Inn Keeper

One day Caesar Augustus, the ruler of the land, passed a law. All the people were told to return to the city from where their family had come, because he wanted to count everyone in his kingdom.

A young couple from Nazareth took a trip to Bethlehem. They had to walk about seventy miles.

When they came to Bethlehem, they were very tired. The streets were full of people. The young man knocked on the door of the motel and asked the manager for a room for him and his wife.

"We are full," the manager said. "We have no more room."

"But, sir, my wife needs a room because she is… she is going to have a baby. Couldn't you find someplace where she can lay down?" the worried husband begged.

"I'm so sorry. All I can offer you is the animal shelter. At least it is warm. Just follow that path; you can't miss it.

The young couple made their way to the hillside stable.

The stable

Jesus was born in a stable. You most likely call it a barn. It is the shelter for donkeys, sheep, and oxen.

Instead of a new baby crib with soft, cuddly blankets, a rough wooden feed box filled with straw was the bed in which Jesus slept.

Jesus was the most important baby who was ever born. He is God's Son. But God did not think that a pretty crib, soft blankets, or a nice house were so important. God had a very special plan.

For God loved the world so much that He gave His only Son, Jesus, so that whoever believes in Him will not perish, but have everlasting life. John 3:16

The Barn Animals

We are the animals who live in the barn. This is a very good place to live if you are an animal. But it is not such a nice place for a baby to be born.

But one night, that is just what happened! A baby was born! We were all snuggled in our straw beds sound asleep, when all of a sudden we heard a baby cry. We ran over and saw a tiny baby lying in our feed box. His mommy and daddy looked so happy.

We felt very special that God had chosen our barn for the place where His Son was to be born.

Mary

My name is Mary.

Something very happy but also very strange happened to me. God sent an angel to tell me that God had chosen me for a very special job. He told me that I was going to be a mommy to a very special baby: Jesus!

Jesus is my son. But He is also God's Son. That makes Him very special not just to me, but to every person in the whole wide world. That means *you*, too. Isn't that awesome?

I am so happy that God chose me for this very special responsibility. I am thankful that Jesus is my *son*, but I am even more thankful that He became my *savior!*

Joseph

My name is Joseph.

God's angel, who spoke to Mary, also spoke to me. He told me that God is Jesus's real father, but He is in heaven. So He wants me to be Jesus's father here on earth. I am so happy God chose me for that role.

I can hardly wait until Jesus is old enough to call me "Daddy." Like Mary, I am thankful that Jesus is my *son*, but I am even more thankful that He became my *savior*.

Baby Jesus

This very special baby is Jesus. He is God's Son.

It is exciting that people all over the world have a birthday party for Him every year on December 25. That is what Christmas is all about!

You remember that He was born in Bethlehem in a barn and that He slept in an animal's feed box. But He did not mind that at all, because He knew that when He would grow up, many people all over the world would invite Him to live in their heart—and that is the best home He could ever want.

He would love to live in *your* heart, too!

The Angel

I am an angel. God created me so that I could do special jobs for Him. Sometimes I bring God's special message to special people on special occasions.

One night, I had the honor of visiting some shepherds who were caring for their sheep on the hills in Bethlehem. But they were so scared when they saw me.

"Do not be afraid," I said to them. "I have good news of great joy for you and all people. Today, in the town of David, a savior has been born to you. He is Christ the Lord. You will find Him wrapped in cloth and laying in an animal's feed box."

At once, they became excited; with big smiles, they ran to Bethlehem to see this new baby.

The shepherds

We are the shepherds, and we feel so very special. Do you know why? Because one dark night in Bethlehem, when we were watching our sheep, we had a very special visitor—an angel! The sky became so bright that we were almost blinded. Wow, were we ever scared!

The angel said, "Do not be afraid," and then told us the most wonderful news for which we had been waiting for hundreds of years— Jesus had been born! We were the *first* people in the whole, wide world to hear the news-breaking story. We got up and ran straight to the barn. Sure enough, there Jesus lay in an animal's feed box. Even as a baby, He was so magnificent that we fell to our knees and worshipped Him.

We told everyone we saw, "O, come, and let us adore Him!"

The Sheep

Sometimes people say that we are not smart enough to take care of ourselves. Maybe so, but we do trust our shepherd to lead us to the right places and to take care of us. We know our shepherd's voice. He keeps us safe and leads us to green pastures, and we follow him.

One night, our shepherds were acting so strange; they ran faster than we could follow to a barn in the hillside of Bethlehem. When we found them, they were acting like sheep who had found the Good Shepherd. And you know what? They *had* found Him!

Jesus was the best shepherd ever. He made them lie down in green pastures, He led them beside still waters, and He restored their soul.

The star

In the beginning, God created heaven and the earth and everything in it. He made the sun, the moon, and the stars on the fourth day. But He saved me for a very special event. When the time was just right, God placed me as that bright new star in the sky to show people that a special king had been born in Bethlehem.

"Twinkle, twinkle little star. How I wonder what you are." I did more than twinkle; I shone so bright in the sky that some men all the way on the other side of the world could see me as I led the way for them to Bethlehem.

The Wise Men

We are the Wise Men who came from the other side of the world. The wisest thing we have ever done was to follow that bright star. It took us almost two years to reach Bethlehem. That is where the star led us. Bethlehem was a little town, and we wondered what could happen here that was so important. But when we saw the little boy, Jesus, we knew right away that He was special and would be a very special king someday.

We kneeled before Him and gave Him our gold, myrrh, and frankincense, but that seemed so small and insignificant. Then we worshiped Him and gave Him the best gift of all; we gave Him our hearts.

Now *that* was really a wise decision! We hope that *you*, too, will worship Jesus, who is the King of kings!

The Camels

We are the camels who carried the wise men to Bethlehem. You recognize us by the humps on our backs. We are very strong and can walk many miles without stopping to rest. We went on a very long journey to come to Bethlehem. We walked for months and months through deserts, across rivers, over hills, and through valleys. We followed a big, bright star.

Our masters, who are kings themselves, were looking for a new king. They brought some very beautiful gifts to give to the new king. We are so proud and happy that we could bring these kings to see *the* King of kings—Jesus.

O Come Let Us Adore Him!!!!!

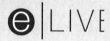 **e|LIVE**

---

listen|imagine|view|experience

AUDIO BOOK DOWNLOAD INCLUDED WITH THIS BOOK!

In your hands you hold a complete digital entertainment package. In addition to the paper version, you receive a free download of the audio version of this book. Simply use the code listed below when visiting our website. Once downloaded to your computer, you can listen to the book through your computer's speakers, burn it to an audio CD or save the file to your portable music device (such as Apple's popular iPod) and listen on the go!

How to get your free audio book digital download:

1. Visit www.tatepublishing.com and click on the e|LIVE logo on the home page.
2. Enter the following coupon code:
   5125-ff8f-9aa0-12a2-736d-510b-dbd5-f468
3. Download the audio book from your e|LIVE digital locker and begin enjoying your new digital entertainment package today!